A Liveright New Writer

In the 1920s Liveright was the first publisher of
William Faulkner, Ernest Hemingway, e.e. cummings,
Eugene O'Neill, Dorothy Parker, Sherwood Anderson,
Hart Crane, Nathanael West, to mention just a few.
Now the new Liveright is once again publishing
the first works of American's most promising young
writers in the Liveright New Writers Series. Its
innovative format provides clothbound quality at
near paperback prices. With this series
Liveright seeks to encourage today's young
writers, provide the best of contemporary writing
for the reading public, and again play a part in
discovering tomorrow's greats.

BLACK ANIMA

N. J. LOFTIS

BLACK ANIMA

LIVERIGHT   New York

MANUFACTURED IN THE UNITED STATES OF AMERICA

Series designed by Betty Binns

For Gayle,
Tony, David, Gregory, and Dawn

Above all, if he were to achieve anything, it was essential that he should banish from his mind once and for all the idea of possible guilt.

KAFKA

For my people thronging Forty-seventh Street in Chicago and Lenox Avenue in New York and Rampart Street in New Orleans, lost disinherited dispossessed and happy people filling the cabarets and taverns and other people's pockets needing bread and shoes and milk and land and money and Something—Something all our own.

MARGARET WALKER

BLACK ANIMA

CHANGES

One

And I sit here
        for five days now
sit here in prison
for running a stoplight in election year
the soiled sunlight from the street
        hard against the vision
piss pouring into latrine
like blood into a butcher's pail

And went on hunger strike
to protest the conditions
        how draft dodgers denied
entry to minimum security
were used as prostitutes
how a man was hung
        with hands tied behind his back
and they called it suicide

And I recognized them
        in the prison library
recognized Malcolm and King

reading from a strange history
the book of our collective dream

"Look," said King
here is Gonga-Mussa
on his pilgrimage to Mecca
this town, his retainers
        60,000 in all
these are the eight camels carrying gold
"And here," said Malcolm
is Cinquez among the founding fathers
        and this figure here
bound in mummy cloth

is your grandfather who is dead
We who are no longer
        yet seem to be
here have the one vision
though in life we were known
        only for our opposition,
the poet among his people
the active man among his books
the single city reached by
        a thousand winding entries

Take this ring
all of whose parts have a common center
joining what's to come
with what has been
        and give it to your bride
whom you shall meet in Africa

And:

___

Two

And I sit here
    sit in the Alamac Hotel
    turning the flux to objects
wondering how your image
survived the gale of history
    signature of all things
I scribble on a rock

    A naked figure flowed
    along the Harlem River
turning, turning in sunlight
weaving the light against it
the waters trying its mouth
    tied a knot in time
not as a moment is
but as a moment might be
    if viewed beyond experience
    near the lighthouse

it fell under sea
but at Wall Street was free

fish nipping in the Bay
picked its fingers clean

Brown legs astride
the straits wide to receive me
exposing unbloomered thighs,
plums for the professor
the wiry hair splayed out
like peacocks' feathers

"Cast down your buckets . . .
    in all things purely social
we can be separate
as the fingers
    yet one as the hand
in all essential to mutual progress"
    these words from Booker T.
    drifted past me
down in Atlanta
I was neither happy nor pained
though since I've wept to think of it
    my lips are dry as dung
my hands are in my lap
and my heart is in my hands

turning, turning, turning
weaving the light against it

These phosphorescent phrases
shrapnels from the lips of time
scribble their signature

across the embalmer's door
Jefferson and his unconscious contradictions
almost floors you
and the French during the Enlightenment,
Voltaire's time, with three slave-galleys
　　Liberté, Egalité, Fraternité
symbols of the Renaissance and the sublime

Yet still you persist
poking a stick in the filthy sands
　　searching for a key
and such meditations as did the Church
consider the raping of slave property
　　bestiality or adultery
　　you cannot resist
Even Lincoln is a bind
from which you can't wiggle free

freeing the slaves in Arkansas, Texas,
Louisiana (except the parishes
　　of Saint Bernard, etc.), Mississippi,
Alabama, Florida, South and North
Carolina, Virginia, Georgia,

but not where he had the authority
In the end you are content
to leave these contradictions
　　these mendacities where they lie
only, and this is the problem,
you are a racing fan
　　gambling on this night mare
on the sly.

———

Still sometimes, when the sun
      sinks behind chestnut trees
and evening settles
      you see the strong faces
of Blacks around a fire
and air turned yellow
and the sound of *Deep River*
      cuts through the undergrowth
drifting down to you

            This music shuffled
            past me in 633
            at the Alamac
            while Miss Brown
            seductively
            exposed her thighs
            her eyes meeting my eyes

And:

Three

Suddenly the woods
were filled with faces,
my heart was in my mouth
and my mouth sinking through my stomach
like Lucifer over the Mississippi;
winds whipping the undergrowth
the heat unbearable
the iron-cold bellow of hooves
hooded figures leaning, staring, leaning
the red dust blotting out the scene . . .
descending a steep flight of steps
through a narrow opening
and the face in the basin was mine
the face like a black death's head

On Sundays we walked up
to the Great Farm House singing
I am going away
I am going away
and music filled the woods

dissipating the holy hush
of ancient evenings. Those same evenings
Mrs. Auld taught me to read
only with the dryness of coke

Those same evenings
when the slaves of Jacob
slaughtered the slaves of Lloyd
boasting their master was better
only longer and the day less bearable

That same evening
Jenkins gave me the root
and said:
        "ain't no man kin whip ya"
and Covey and me fighting
in a cotton patch
until the dawn collapsed

                Jericho, Jericho, Jericho
                and the walls come tumbling down

"I have, may it please the court
a few words to say.
I intended clearly
to make a clean thing of the matter
as I did last spring
when I went into Missouri
and there took slaves
without the snapping of guns

———

I never intended murder
or even treason, or destruction of property
or inciting slaves to rebellion
or making an insurrection"

"Had I intervened in similar manner
(And you know well I've admitted
this thing, admitted it was proven fairly)
in behalf of the rich
the powerful, the indolent—
that we call great—
or in behalf of their friends,
the near great and parasites,
this court would have deemed it right
would have deemed it worthy of respect
and not for punishment"

O Jericho, Jericho, Jericho

".... But for the storm, you see,
we would have reached Havana
in two, three days at most,
but from the calm skies that followed,
the queer stillness should have been
a signal, the brutes fell upon us
with machete and marlinspike.
It is a dismal sight to see those
savages kill (we murder from necessity,
they to appease some primitive will) .
Cinquez hacking that poor mulatto down

---

and our men's butchered bodies spread
over the slippery decks."

And the walls came tumbling down

"The steel sky darkened to the north
and the bloodsmeared sunset
stretched across the west
the dry thunder pealing
in the intervening calmness
and suddenly the clouds folded back
and I saw the Black armies
and the armies of Whites
engaged in spirited struggle . . .
when the vision finally left me
        there was only the enormous silence
and the blood upon the corn.

"And I saluted them as they came up
saluted Sam, Nelson, Will and Jack.
And I asked Will why he had come there
and Will replied, his life was worth
no more than others, his liberty as dear.
And we first murdered Travis
a good master as masters go,
and his wife and family
(later Will and Henry went back
        for the baby)

"And bashed Mrs. Newson aside
the head, for the blade was dull

---

and Will dispatched her
and likewise dispatched Mr. White
trembling in a cotton patch . . .
I looked upon his fiendlike face
with its broad features and negroid nose
and my blood ran cold."

turning, turning, turning

Ascending the seventeenth floor
of the Alamac by an elevator
to the mortuary school . . .
all is suddenly come
nothing rests at all
nothing but the mark upon my door
of the burning hand of the embalmer

Four

The sky, rare sight in the city, gliding down in rough waves with Henry, the first black angel since the Italians took over heaven, shaking a fist full of thunderbolts, planted firmly between two clouds, directly on the deeds, mine, I mean. If there are two things I hate it's the earth and the sky, said Watt, but said nothing about the sea. You'd think it would make him sick, always shining out there at the edge of the sand, unfurling its blue tongue on the beach. No, no that's a reverse aesthete, saying naughty things because they're interesting. But can we be, free I mean, beyond the province of hot breaths clashing and the subtle pressure urging us on again. He, i.e. the Father of Israel, is always trying to give us our freedom and we are always trying to give it back—Dostoevsky. Corollary: He is always trying to give us our freedom while Caesar always acts as though it were intended for him. Thus the necessity for a dialectic is evident. As long as there are abandoned fields to be tilled tomorrow by someone you recognize as you, revolution is not a hope but a fact looked forward to. Until then we render to both Church and Caesar their soiled penny, or at least two sides of the same penny in view of the recession and this being an election year.

A loud crash and in the intervening blackness the credits flashed impatiently across the screen, sparrows fluttering fly toward a tree away from the disaster. Finally the ambulance arrives on the scene. Surprised by so much intensity, yet secretly pleased by the sudden surge of energy and the uncontrollable, if misunderstood, ecstasy of abruptly being released from fear, we walk like Donne's sublunary lovers among spectators. True, a certain instinctive dislike of suffering snatched from us something akin to pity. Still, neither the two heads protruding through the window-shield of the jackknifed automobile, nor the gradual realization that we were dead altered the immense sense of freedom we felt. Perhaps only this freedom is real, the sudden release from the body without the illusory constraints of karma urging us on again. Part of the cycle . . .

Ramakrishna Mission Lectures
Thursdays and Fridays on The Bardo
Thodal and Hindu Philosophy. Sunday
service 11:00 A.M.

Passing this same place more than three years. First time I noticed it. E.S.P. Maybe I called it into being. Ineffable power of seeing. Once in Gretz. Wind sweeping in out of the mystic north. Brown of hayfield hard against the sky. Jewish she was, onyx-eyed. Hair a mess of snake tails. Girl, gon make you lose your religion. Grandmother before she died. Grandmother didn't lie. Face half hidden under checkered kerchief, calling the Shabbaz queen. Night of yellow vertigo discussing Hindu philosophy while sipping

---

17

lukewarm sugarless tea. Old scene. The gale of today with her long windy legs assaults me now. What was her name? Met at party. Coming when she's leaving. Chance meeting. That sort of thing. The voice drifting like ashes over the Ganges. Choir of Virgins. Couldn't tell him apart. Not a queen, but what a queen might be if pressed beyond the border of sexuality. Sleeping in trees. Monkeys making sorrowful noises. Bringing memories. The time when he was Rama. The Monkey God. His spine spreading downward two inches. From his detached position he might have seen details that we, engaged in the business of being, might overlook. For instance, all roads lead to the same city. *Exits* and *entrances* are basically the same, depending on which way you're coming. Even his admonishing against women and gold shouldn't be taken too literally. What's important is getting beyond matter to what it means. To become a huckster, or dealer in fake furs need not avert us from the Ground of Being. Even Freud in one of his dazzling masturbatory fantasies saw the striptease of the ego. The cumbersome mental furniture removed from a privileged position in mental cavity and placed on the lawn like a housewife doing spring cleaning. The protean wilderness of the *id* rising before it. And another landscape, the narrow constructs of the super-ego receding through a chink in the side of a cliff. What was her name? Fine brown frame. That ought to take me back a bit. Shit, shit, shit, shit. Name? Wendy, no, started with a G., Gwendolyn. No, too German. The past is history, the future is becoming the past through me. I am only a drunken bridge suspended between the disentangled corpses of yesterday and those to be. Eighty-ninth Street. Five stops more. Then rose out on the great dancing stage Plotinus, snapping imaginary ego-fetters and impressing us all with his ability to keep in balance what we'd thought to be duality. What we had seen as the self, God, and the collective will, in fact was the holy trinity. Through the supervening declivity of ego, I am table, table is chair, chair is see. See what I mean? You out there, hey, sparrow, through the soiled bus window, I am you and you are a butterfly's shadow, lightly eluding each passerby. Lilacs are in bloom. At least I presume what's blooming are lilacs. What do I know of such things? I hereby abolish all landscapes. Only ideal landscapes are real. The equatorial sunbeams spread out like high Afros of tall native girls bent over wooden basins washing clothes. The circular movement of dancers syncopating to the beat of congo. The Great Mother beneath yellow parasol, with massive breasts extended to abundant lap, eating an ear of corn. While above, the moon makes angry faces at the midnight sun. My stop. Shall I descend the stair? Do I:

Five

No, no Shakespeare not your gloomy melancholy. *To be or not to be* is a kink you've cleverly cast in the body's machine which takes everything in and shits it all out again, a sideshow like midget-wrestling or fat ladies rubbing bellies to distract us from the real tragedy. That shadowy being we see ranting before us on the stage is too much like us to be taken as mere "play," and, perhaps,

too much like you, busy contemplating the visible reality, while a mindless destiny that a star-haunted heaven has written in indecipherable calligraphy, a heaven lamenting with convulsive stars, has gently attached itself to you from without.

It is all too proximate to be funny, or merely amusing. Today a musical would be made to wean us from its piercing sting, the dread terror of the thing, truth too real to be ignored, too protracted to be acted upon. Fortunately, the dead only return to us in grade "B" movies, dreams, or poets' imaginings, permitting us the luxury of postponing true perception of reality indefinitely, until another life, if need be, or to twist it into a shape that agrees with our fantasies. Still, suppose a bright billboard appeared in the sky reading: THIS IS YOUR IDENTITY. Oh, how I would delight to see the homosexual and the he-man delighting in what a homosexual and a he-man should be. Lacking this clear certainty, the surety of birds of passage cracking open hostile skies as a crack goes through a cup, we abandon our true being, being existing solely for itself, not needing the other to confine or define it from without, being all essence without a rim.

It is time to take inventory. You've packed the luggage and left the key next door. Plane at eleven. Auden's for tea. What time is it? Three. Time to take inventory. The Library at six. Leaving there by taxi. It is time,

time to examine the very ground on which we walk, to examine the room settling about your shoulders at afternoon, to examine it through and through: to see. But even this is illusory if you cannot annihilate the subtle dependencies that anticipate the object seen, surmising all its fate, its character and mental state without once staring it face to face, or noticing its body's distinct from the mask it placed on its head to deceive you.

Until that frontier where you can see the dizzy depths from which earth is always uprooting itself, where momentary and cosmic meet, connecting the simple and transitory "me" with eternity, you must awake nightly with the shriveled head of a limp dream, you must content yourself not simply with being, but swapping shapes with the things surrounding you, for how else shall you know them, since the ground is corroded where you might have detached yourself from the muddle of images attacking you and surveyed the whole, the "To-Ti," from its vague beginning in history right down to the present uncertainty.

You must complete the death begun in you, plunging to hell, if that's what you must do, before you can release yourself from that protean empathy with your locality, before you stand anew at the end of dreams on the very Ground of Being from which the roses spring, not just a point on the ring but the ring itself.

But all that is far from where you are right now, walking down Broadway toward the subway, the scrawny tree becomes you, not decking itself out like queen, but exchanging its being with yours until the piss pours on you that errodes the bark away, and the cool winds seem to tear off your limbs.

You are the tree that is pissed upon and the dog that pisses, demanding red meat three times a day, your right to lie where and with whom you wish, shelter when sunlight makes a pyre of the leaves, a human hand to scratch your belly when it brings delight. Yes, you know your rights. The moon and other heavenly bodies no longer concern you, who bay only when human kindness turns to aggression, only at the demeaning invectives against your breed, indeed, against everything dog denotes: "doggone," "dog take ya," "dog damn." What you're asking is a reversal of things, to be treated not as men, but as gods, so that the

before the rising sun.
I came here when slavery was young. . . .

The sun fell gently, Gentlemen,
across my corduroy shoulders
the day that I was crucified
bleeding in my strophes

The day that W. D. Howells
        wrote, "I find most
charming . . . the pieces where
he studies the mood
and the traits of his race"

I died a double death today
I read the thing, racing between
sky and lobby, unseen
driving my elevator machine
the recognition so near, grown light years away
        I wanted to scream
I wanted to tear open my breast and say:
        Look, This is My body. See.

And Wystan said to me
        on Saint Mark's Place
As afternoon trembled like coffee
in a cup, Wystan Auden
        said, "a Catholic Worker
and friend in women's prison
heard a whore exiting to shower
declaim my lines:

---

thousands have lived without love,
but few without water.

"The irony almost jolts you to the floor
but who could imagine
who could imagine creating for a whore"

We are neither gods nor saints—
to stink of poetry shows a lack
        of taste, to use our
privileged place to justify
too human sins, a lack
of principle within.

Beware of both the aesthete,
who like Yeats,
tells pretty lies because appealing
and the unacknowledged legislators of state
        who confound their function
        with that of the secret police

Take this golden pen with scarab's head
        the boys at the British Museum
recognizing it will guide you through
the secret wing of the dead

            Here, take:

Seven

I came down the steamship stair
    with my heart in my hands
and my hands in my pockets
my antennae quivering in purled air,
hatred so thick you could slice it.

And the compressed atmosphere
beat about me like tiny wings
    and sang diaphanously:

        Bur Bur Bureeghardt
        Bur Bur Bureeghardt

Came home to America having seen
the Nile quick with crocodiles
bathed in the blue Ganges
    talked with Plato
on the steps of the Academy
and watched crass Caesar
in the rape of Italy

Came home a sort of seventh son
        neither Teuton nor Mongolian,
        seeing the truth of things
having the gift of second sight
knowing the wrong from the right

But oh the twoness pains you so
two beings make my bed
        I go through the world
like a hammer with two heads
neither seeing nor seen
neither being for myself
nor wholly what they want me to be

                Thou are not dead, dear Lord,
                But flown afar
                Thou are not dead, dear Lord,
                But flown afar

The light blazed through crypt forest
        along its way
and the voice of Bone crying
in the wildernesses of intellectual
lethargy, "What have you given,
Burghardt, What empathy have
you given your people?"

What I gave will not be spoken of
        in my eulogy
deeds done out of love
others done out of hatred of strife
When I might have stayed in Germany

What did I give, you ask me?
My life, my life, my life,

Thou art not dead, dear Lord
Lord, thou art not dead

Eight

And one day Hughes said
    "I've known rivers ancient as the world and older
than the
        flow of human blood in the veins"

thus cutting across time's withershins
the combustible leaves of *Crises*
    like the processional reds and golds
    of autumn ablaze in the crypt forest

Atropos cutting the thread
    weaving the light against it
and Rosy living in London said
to her reclining Sappho
"I told Langston he'd be dead at sixty
if he didn't stop eating"

        the swollen corpse adrift
           on the black tide
        time's knot tied and untied

as it rose and fell
the half-submerged belly
blown out like a sail

Time sifts the wheat from the chaff
and the rat from the wheat:
and Tolson first traced the course
where the rainbow arched to its source
plunging to the pitch and pith of things
containing more of alchemy than a witch's sabbath

The shadow swimming vaguely
in the Library's light
gathering the gold against them
a few friends and you break bread
attended by all the resident dead
that line the bookstalls
that's what poetry is (Auden)
or maybe it was Lenny Horn,
a bridge between the dead and the unborn
"So you are going to Egypt
to resurrect Ikhnaton's tomb"
The words pass through you
falling on a stony place where nothing blooms
Outside, the saffron sunlight swims
toward you in concentric circles
as day goes down

Then Chesnutt, let his ladder down,
down into the leper commune
his mind shattered by the gale

of images, picking and choosing identities
as at a rummage sale

You memorized your lesson well
pointing it all out in detail
        to others in your company
trying to tell them how Mphahlele
and Spender unwittingly (perhaps)
were cuddled by the CIA

Imagine climbing all your childhood
toward some promontory
        where you dreamed the white cliffs
        shot up out of the bickering spray
only to find when arriving there
what you dreamed had gone away
        or perhaps never existed
and what remains is only a cheap
and mean province open to all comers

You would make of that paltry place
the thing you always dreamed
who else but Mphahlele could praise
        Joseph C. so openly
thereby renouncing his birthright
on the banks of the Nile
and swap the sculptured beauty of Nefertiti
swap it for the bulges of Queen Vicky

Imamu (LeRoi) saw it all six
        years ago at the Black Arts
        before fools fell upon the place

"Your gonna have to forget
      everything taught you down in Tennessee"
Malcolm was just dead and maggots
spreading their whiteness over his cold body

What whiteness shall we add
to this whiteness like sterile clouds
      bellowing dryly over the Pentagon?
      I'll tell you
the whiteness of fear
flashing across the hunter's face
when he is no longer hunter but quarry

Were it not for the glory
said Marlowe, were it not for the glory . . .
      Makers of history they.
      We, those to whom it happens.
Straw men bending
when the gale blowing gently
shakes the wheat from the chaff

On the banks of the Seine
      the spell shall be broken
Prospero's wand shattered in two
      and tossed out to sea.
Yes a tempest is afoot
      that he won't survive so easily

            Caliban! Caliban!
               Blow your horn, man

                              TAXI TAXI TAXI

Nine

Spiked cadillacs with silver teeth
Miss Black America
in blond wig
     waves at us
from chauffeured limousine

Stereos blasting behind closed
     loan shop windows
Black volcanic rhythms
Black music
     Black soul
into sterile cocaine heaven

       O think think
       'bout what you tryin'
       to do to me

Cruising through Harlem in a gypsy cab
     for the other taxis

were on strike that year
the darkness syncopating
turning, writhing, stretched
on a cross of lassitude.

      Half watts of celluloid
      dread whistling down
      to you

Aretha is at the Apollo
Black soul sister
whose Veiled tribal sounds
      shattered the mask
      of Athena
Aretha is at the Apollo
screening on a shield
the dreadful prospects of tomorrow

      You'd better
      think, think
      O you'd better
      think

Her euphoric therapy
      only appeasing distress
even between her breaths
      hearts fluttering
      in calcified cavity

---

the panic in the abdomen
the Negro syndrome
revives again
        squads of heroin
        under long-sleeved shirts
circulate through the arteries
        faster than
        the IRT

Is it you, Federico Garcia
walking these mean streets
        where a skyful
        of visionary birds
strike at you
along the corners of fear
You who taught us to sing
the poet among his people
        the multitude
        with its king
beautiful, graceful, Garcia
your sex transfixed into a flower's

        Your rumor reaches me
        Your rumor reaches me

It is the hour of the wolf

        I am going away
        I am going away

the airport nearly deserted
the city unmasked
by a barrage of lights
lies naked

swing low sweet cadillac
swing low sweet cadillac

It is time to begin again, Mrs. Epstein
you who are perishing
the revolution is at hand
    I, Diamond Katambo
    leading linguist
at the Institute for Black Speech
see the mirror cracked
    in the hallway
and the blood upon the wall
I see the ruin of all space
    and hear the sound
    of crumbling masonry
    Listen!

Now once again with feeling
"Baby"
No, no, your voice sounds too deceiving
"Ba-By"
Ah, Mrs. Epstein, Mrs. Epstein
you see being a nigger's
    not as easy as it seems
We who were dead are now living

You who were living
    are now dying

        Boom!   Boom!   Boom!   Boom!   Boom!
        drop,   drop,   drop,   drop,   drop
        Boom!   Boom!   Boom!   Boom!
        drop,   drop,   drop,   drop,
        Boom!   Boom!
        drop,
        drop

Bing! Bing! *No smoking please*
the bell in the interior
releases the night mares
    from the post
the plane climbing skyward
leaves the dead concerns
of the earth behind

      swing low sweet cadillac
      I'm going away and ain't
      never coming back

Pen my suit-coat pocket,
ring gleaming, burning, gleaming
    ordering the air around it
the plane unbuttoning the sky
    the void jetting by.

What's that face in the distance
    a manned missile?
    a cloud formation?
man standing between the reach of sky

      O pilot, pilot me
      over life's tempestuous sea

nearer it comes
nearer my God to thee

      turning, turning, turning
      weaving the light against it

There's no place to hide down there
"Hide me," cried the desert
"We're burning, too," cried the rocks

HELL

Ten

And we went down
    down under the ground
    under the town
    down in the catacombs
descending the steep stairs
    endlessly, so that where
    we were was only an opening
a chink in the darkness's armor
shadows flooding space the light vacated

Came at last to the stony landing
    where Sibby, Dame Sybil Leek,
    was selling candles and tea
And Sibby said, *"Prenez Monsieur,*
l'obscurité des catacombes est
égale seulement à l'obscurité de la vie,
    The darkness of these catacombs
    is equal only to the obscurity of life."*

And the darkness sailed across our skin
silently as flesh filing from the bone

the candlelight flickering
often disappearing from sight
before the pitchness put back the light
dead footfalls echoing through the halls
lizards triggering across the ground

And the bright bones navigating into view
illuminating portraits painted on human skin.

"Voici," said our guide, "is one
dedicated to the sweetness and purity
that we, the meek, bloated with hypocrisy,
    only speak of privately
    or write about in books
here's the lord and master
of this place, *Mon Führer*

"And here, his right-hand man
Who, twenty years after the *Führer*'s death
    devised a master plan to carry
    out his will in the modern way.
Though his bones are here before you
the body of Dr. Skinner still walks
    the earth, still haunts the land
in search of fame which he snatches where he can"

The darkness unfolded in sheets
a few feet at a time
    the spider light lifting its legs
    devoured the blackness in small bites
and we, walking in harmless bands

like some procession of the dead
      without flutes' swirl or knell of drum

And behind me I heard one whose
      voice I recognized, and turning
      in surprise I said,
"Marge, Marge Dixon, what, you here?
Where can your trickster husband be
      is he still selling used cars
      down in Cincinatti?"

      And she replied,

"Oh, darling, how have you been
      how have you been
      it's so nice to meet a friend
when one is traveling
There's so little time in the States
to meet new people, make new dates
      the morning sweeps by so quickly
      sweeps by like a broom
pushing us into afternoon
where we sit sipping tea
      wondering what the morning's meant
then night falls like a guillotine

"Dick's doing well
      had the Vice Presidency
      since '63
when he sold the same cadillac
to eighteen colored families
The company,

---

naturally, applauds his labor
and his honest industry"

And came suddenly to a clearing
with the washed-out glare
of electric lights
the red sign reading:

ARRÊT:
L'EMPIRE DE LA MORT

And the bones aglow
stretched in neat rows
and singing diaphanously
the death's-heads setting sail
floating languidly toward the ceiling
seem to be floating
so intense their stillness

"Et ici," said our guide
"Ici you have the sacred remains
of the most famous names in history
Here is Hugo, here's Baudelaire
whose perversity and flair
have been a beacon for modern man

"Here is Josephine. See!
still lovely even in death
and those bones glowing
with such intensity

---

that seem, being dead, to command authority
 these bones were her master's,
 the Emperor,
not one here can say if I lied"

And Ruby, Ruby Cheeks, who also
 numbered in the dead,
asked me to take her to the Library
for drinks when she got out in spring
"I've got sixty prints, she said,
sixty times I've been inside
 but never has any stretch
 left me so depressed."
Likewise Mary came to me
and tore my heart out of its cavity
 and devoured it where it lay
 still keeping the body's time,
Mary Harper, hardly the mother of J.C.,

Who started mainlining after she
and her baby
 (which she conceived in rape
 at only seventeen)
were forced by her daddy
to abandon the house
 when she refused him entry
through the swollen gates

Mary, who was laid by Ruby
 while trying to suck some kindness
 from her granite breast,

Whom Cobra loved and faithfully
    each night tried to deflower
who, so sweet and delicate a thing,
started developing claws
to survive the jungle of her desires

Not that her desire knows perversity,
    knows perversity yet,
      nor loves anything
but the pure and unwatched-over
    poetry of her own loveliness

Mary, whose eyes lifted tombstones
    like the million Marys
measuring out their snowy doom each day
circulating inside their lymph
    like the Broadway Express

    Who:

Eleven

"Ain't committed no crime but being Black
    an' assertin' my identity,"
so spoke Brenda (Butch) Carter
lover of Lesbos and Sappho

Busted in '69 by a 'blind' cop
    on two counts of pimping
    and mainlining
"Ninth time in," protested Ruby
    "and she only twenty-three
Parolled provisionally a year ago
her flock fled, fled to a bitch
    gone AC, DC,
burning at both ends
Considered going straight, screwing men,
    when a warrant fell again.

"And the judge,
    a Long Island housewife
    whose eyes erected altar lights
    of visionary paradise,

the judge offered to set her free
when Butch jumped to her feet
  and cried, 'Hell, naw do your duty,
give me bed and board.' "

Similarly Erma Jackson once remarked,
  "It ain't heaven, but you
get three squares a day
and all the bitches you can lay."

   These recollections came to me
hearing the chain's sonorous hissing
the men in hipcoats dragging
  the boat behind,
  our guide, an ex-con out of Pigalle
holding forth proudly

    "Vous avez ici, Monsieur et Madame

"Vous avez les égouts de Paris
les plus connus du monde.
Voici, vous avez l'égout
  pour Madelaine.
  Et ici, sont les égouts
pour tout l'ouest de Paris

    Regardez! See!

A gray river rat swam past me
shifting its slimy body
    astride the drift,
the sewers stinking like a soap factory,
the water breaking warmly
about me as I watched her
sitting in the boat behind

The recognition fleeting across her face
escaped through the scissors of a smile
    then the fierce contour
of her visage tightened like a fist . . .
This game enforced smirks
Yet no black-sailed ship ever dreamed
such starless piracy as I.

Cleopatra, Nefertiti, Black Eurydice
there is no name wild enough to tame
    the foudroyant flutter
of a single one of her lashes
no hawk that soars from east
    to west
to stay the pneumatic fury
of her trembling breast

And as the guide said,
    "Le tour des égouts est terminé,"
    desire mixed with memory
broke wide from my side
shipwrecking where she sat

No Babylonian prophecy of doom

could efface the wonder of her effigy
    striding behind me step for step
the windless stairs unwinding into day.

Turning, she had gone away

Twelve

I was just musing about the British Museum
        thinking on Angela and her plight
        when the spirit came to me
and I said, "Plato, Plato Hathmore
director of Public Planning
back in Baltimore

            "And Plato said

'Ex-director you mean
        since you, head swelling with images
of former welfare clients
wrote those nasty things
against me and the board,
        the bloody bastards,
        heaped insults on me
and for all that I produced
gave me nothing but abuse

'forgetting it was me
in my Model Cities plan

that made the woman
equal to the man
and gave the rich and poor
a place together
tumbling the highborn
and giving to the people
what they'd waste

'Those that they should praise
they treat like crooks,
no, worse than crooks, like shit.
But enough of it, 'Doctor,'
they'll find these arguments
in your book.
I've been instructed
seeing that scarab's head on your pen
to take you to the library
to your newfound friend.' "

And I recognized them sitting there
sitting in the Museum library
recognized Wright and Tolson
Pushkin and Yeats, recognized 'the swells'
assembling a strange book
the burning leaves of hells

And Pushkin said, "Here's Homer's hell,
the archetype is Egyptian
where the sun fell
over Luxor scribbling its dread command
in Ikhnaton's brain.
And this is the hell of Dante

---

took the day
sinking our black-sailed ships
        and with the women had his way
before you sent him onrushing
back to Tennessee"

        And Frantz said

"You have come face to face
        with your destiny
like the Egyptian dead and his effigy
you shall know all
and *All* is everything

But for the time being
content yourself with momentary
        snatches of reality, remembering
as you walk heedless through the city streets
even socialism must enrich the many
not simply deprive the privileged few
beware the hazards of technology
what Skinner wants is a human zoo."

Fourteen

Sing in me muse, Mary,
    Mother of Sorrow,
seduced nightly in your cell
by Cobra whose clitoris swells
    like a black blimp
sing while I tell of Mrs. Green
far from the City of Hope
    and Mrs. Spaulding
whose caseworker fell upon her
like cloud-gathering Zeus
leaving her a bundle for her abuse

Sing while I tell of old wrongs
    and new wrongs
the mad whore plunging
her foot through glass door
Harlem hidden by
    huge heroin sheets
niggers beating each other in the streets

And we came to the ship
and Frantz found a quarter

---

and put it in the slot
the boat tossed and bucked
tearing off sharp chunks of sky
        giant fans whipping
        the water in pools
plastic Odysseus at ship's stern
barking commands until the voice died
and Frantz put another quarter in the ship's side

"This is Homer's Hell"
        said Frantz, "the hell of antiquity
See the black ship breaking under sea
the small fishes swimming by
        the dead souls down below
clamoring to see what they left behind
who today would be terrified
        of such a thing
fortunate to get from summer
into the next spring
without being mugged in broad daylight
and our bodies drawn and quartered

"Raised in the ghetto
sickened daily by the sight of slaughter
        such scenes have little novelty for you.
Man has improved on killing
as he's grown older
more given to despair
more bored by living

        "Let us pass on
        there is little to shock you here."

_____

Fifteen

Broken the great floodgates
the godly sea uprooting tents,
  earth churned, trees broken,
  a maniac storm of leaves,
rain falling in cold sheets
though no rain wets a single thing
the conveyor walkway winding
into day of glass dome

And I saw them there
  saw Malcolm and King
  carved on an urn
greeting each other hand in hand
and saw Kennedy (Bobby) carved
in stone, sculptured so lifelike
a sweet lament, most sacred
  of all Sorrow's daughters,
showed me her dark declivities,
saw him there also, Marcus
the magnificent, Marcus Garvey

And Sibby said, *"Prenez Monsieur,*
l'obscurité des tombes, l'obscurité de la vie . . .

To be more fully what you are
forget what you meant to be
        the broken wall, the heap
        of smoldering victory lights
that time cannot appease
the city that you carry from place
to place like a dread disease:
what's ceased to be cannot offend,
strip naked in your clay
        and dance, dance, dance, I say

Still, since where you're going is where you've been
        relive the grief and pain
Once more, consume it all
before setting out for what you came
under the hostility of southern skies

                and came to an opening
                where birds attacked each other
                diving into daylight
                down

A place shaped like a football field
sands smoldering underfoot
nude bathers walking around in rings
        And I recognize the poet
admiring himself in his bikini
and I said, "Mr. Elicut, what a sad
day for poetry, what are you doing
        in this dismal city?"

And Mr. Elicut said, "When I lived
above I wrote only of sin and body's
contamination, now I'm forced to feel life's fascination
　　you'll find Wally in the rear
still a stick-in-the-mud, poor dear.
Excuse me, I see a swinging chick
Think I'd like to meet, got to do my thing
you know what I mean, old bean."

　　　　Leaving
We wandered across the sands
to where the infield began
　　in baseball season
　　and on the green coolness
of the diamond saw him standing
next to Nasser and De Gaulle
and when he saw me came and pulled
my nose, turning to his company
　　and cried, "Look,
see, I'm his granddaddy!"

　　　　And grandpa said,
"I'm glad you've gotten your degree,
your grandmother, too, is tickled silly
　　yet for the past few years
you've burned the hearts that loved you
like a mad incendiary
listen grandson, friend, listen, listen
you can't make light bulbs from starry dreams
　　negating your responsibility each
time some Dido, pregnant with your baby,
sends herself to hell and goes on welfare.

———

The winter hawk destroys
  the toys of summer
  do a trusty day's work
join lotus and machine
for our sake's sake, sing."

        And as the Twilight hammered its shafts
        into the brightness of afternoon

I saw her standing there
standing at the edge of the green
the light engulfing her
swimming down to her
    in her transparent negligee
outstripping soft circles of evening
invading like a predestined piracy
her face rising like a black balloon
before it went away.

Sixteen

Walking through windless orchards
    inside museum's secret wing
    along the gravel path
where water trickles over the breaker
discussing what we'd seen
came to a red door marked:

        BEWARE:
        DANTE'S INFERNO

And the chilled blast almost floored me
the blue-black cold
    like a year of Januaries
cries from inside ascending to crescendo
the siren hissing of chains
the unmentionable odor of rotten meat
    burning my nostrils
and forcing the blue vomit to my teeth.

        The stockyards of Chicago

High vaulted ceiling extending fifty feet
the wooden walkway laid in circularly.
        Only instead of pigs
naked white legs dangled and kicked
        bound to meathooks upside down
        blood rushing to brain
chained hands writhing into prayer
moaning, screaming, driving you insane

As the bodies came twisting in their chains
        and pausing momentarily
        eager Blacks stood in line
stood on platform, waiting
waiting to take their turns
with butcherknife slashing
        a foot-long cut in jugular vein
and the blood jettisoning
in sheets to ground
like a horse pissing in latrine

And as one of the screaming effigies
        of humankind came kicking round
        on the slaughter-line
a small Black woman raced
from her place behind and cried:
"Hold everything, Mr. Silver's mine."
And with the butcherknife
        made a door in his throat
        for the blood to exit by
And Frantz said:
"Mr. Silver was that lady's landlord
an absentee who tried to force her family

---

to vacate, first with eviction
though her rent was paid up-to-date
then cutting off the heat in the worst
cold wave seen, her baby caught pneumonia
as in a dream ceased its residency on earth

"Still she survived the winter
but never knew another spring
the building mysteriously set afire
and she and her other three were burned alive."

And hearing that awful history
I cried, "Cut the bastard
one for me."
And Frantz said, "Easy, you'll get
your turn, this vision that you see
is no other-worldly prophecy
but a preview of the future
the men that run this blood factory
won revolutionary victories in the street."

We left by the door through which we came
only where the orchard had been

Greasy tropical trees were stinking
with rotten fruit, monkeys dangling
from black branches holding mirrors
shearing their shades from the leaves
a crocodile, one lake of lizard,
crawling lazily along the ground

Came to a clearing where rows of Whites
tied to swollen stakes watched helplessly,

fat drops of sweat falling
like English pennies to the soil,
the Black men gathered in groups,
gathered around cages of river rats
trapped for these festivities.

And Frantz said:

"These disgusting bodies that you see
        in life were politicians
who assuming a thousand different shapes
disseminated hatred and strife.
The fame has come full circle
        for the brothers that you see
                are laying odds who will be
the first to exchange his shape
for a river rat's."

And as Fanon was still filling in the facts
A rat scrambled from the cage
shrieking, turning aimlessly in a rage
        before choosing its victim
and affixing its teeth along the cheek
with such fury that the man fell
motionless to the ground

And gradually the rat's head spread
as the man's contracted beady eyes
        two feet turning into four
merciless and tiny, losing the power of speech.
Frantz and I beat a swift retreat
as I had grown quite sick

We found ourselves on a dirty artery
between the river and the city dump
        when naked figures came stumbling
        over the bumpy road
balancing barrows filled with shit

                And Frantz said:

"Catch one returning with barrow empty
and see if he dare admit his infamy"

                And I said:

"Hey John, John D., you see
all your stealing ended in futility"
        And he said, "Woe, woe is me
from shit I came unto shit I have returned again.
But worse than not having money
I grew accustomed, I've grown accustomed to this smell
        that's the hell of the place.
Tell Rocky a place awaits him here"

                When:

Seventeen

And we sat down on the docks—
exiled from Babylon a second time
saw the slow sad dance of
the dead man turning
    turning in sunlight—
weaving the light against him

Heard the double swirl of a saxophone
then the soft flair of a trombone
as one rose sadly from underground
    black as the absence of day
and set blithely about his way

And some English chap from Chelsea
damn near bowled him over
    didn't see the bloke
and the Black man fell upon him
damn near battered out his brains
before he caught himself,
    the honkey half dead,

---

restrained himself, remembering his invisibility
and the bloke hadn't seen 'em.

And when back home underground
where he lives rent-free
flinching electric lights
        from the electric-light company;
and listen passively to Miles
wrapped in a gray veil of reefer smoke
till day came up

                Come to me
                wherever you done been
                Come to me, my brother, my friend

Then the music drifted down to me
the spade at the trumpet
        set his head aswirl
as the gypsy flame flickered
and swayed, ebbing the night away

And he went down to Picadilly
bored out of his skull
to try and find some bitch
        to take the boredom away
to suck the froth of ennui
from the tip of his budding tree

                Come to me
                wherever you done been
                Come to me, my lover, my friend

Night, night, night
    mad inexhaustible night
wrapped in scarlet and muslin
pulsating like maggots
    contracting and expanding
as they eat the dead bullocks
the heroin death eating
    his breath away
gnawing at his armpits
as it traveled through his veins
faster than the underground

    And:

Eighteen

You are at the end of your journey
      your guide has departed
and you go through the London streets
cocked like a gun

All those images rush on you
      as you sit in some pub
hear the tinkering piano
murder the music you love.
Your ring is in your pocket
your golden pen in your lapel.
Well, you were not the first rat
to be seen swimming
toward a sinking ship

In the end you file those images away
until you discover what they've meant
and where it is you've really been.
      Nothing you have seen
has changed anything because you have not changed,

---

not the evening falling like a guillotine
around Mrs. Dixon's porphyry shoulders
nor the morning rising to greet you
each time you look in Mary's eyes

You must put this hell behind you
remembering this poised self
        that you once were
that might have proven something
        yet never proved
that never knew the midnight of her smile.
Let that content you and be gone, make do,
You cannot look upon dawn's fawn flesh
where a moonlight city stands
dismembered as bones in a butcher's can

BIRTH AND REBIRTH

Soft whirls of sunlight fondle your face as the dawn rises to greet you from her place dropped over the black mountain like a rosy necklace. You leave this hellhole from Barcelona, dry winds whipping in out of the mystic north, the ship enclosed in a mastaba of heat, seagulls diving and retreating through cellophane windows of sea. The chained sea itself. Phantasmal seasounds grating like the steatopygia of waddling flesh.

You must begin here at the beginning, if it is a beginning, risking everything, even death, if you are to escape the death already taken root in you. The ship tosses softly by high cliffs

churning churning churning
          weaving the light against it

Not even the light, but the new gleam nourishing itself in the womb of sky before bursting the floodgates bringing forth the morning lovely and lean.

See, the dawn's tiny footprints have left tracks on the stars that the inquisitive can trace back to beginning, even before sin exchanged her innocent and subtle hues for the scarlets we know so well, back to womb's darkness swelling the bowels of regaling evening breaking wide from the enormous seascape on which you calmly go.

There is no loveliness to be added to this loveliness, no chuckling midnight bright enough to efface this broad sea-smile. All this contents you, lifting you out of the whiteness from which you came, transporting you to new domains where the glory will be less private, the pain more bearable, and the landscape more friendly, like a gust of rain when the dryness has scorched your lips. You cannot restrain that old refrain pulsating in your brain, nor cast quite behind you the salt tears pumping to your eyes as it sails into the mind:
Brothers and Sisters pray

> And help me to drive
> old Satan away

nobody knows the trouble I've seen

The sea is a serpent-god, its coils convulsing as it goes flapping on its way dragging memories into day of things you've seen and felt and things you've felt and seen. Your first glance at Auden toppling up the stairs of Saint Mark's Place and disappearing into the black door of eternity. The Mississippi rolling gently on as you wave from cotton-fields at passers-by, DuBois dying in Ghana, Baraka at the Black Arts. Booker T. in Atlanta selling us back into slavery.

You have seen it all and there's been so much to see. Not seen, perhaps, but been as in a dream where there is no distinction between your feelings and those of people close to you. It was more than just empathy, it was abandoning your being to become what you might have been. You felt that way the first day you met Mary and later showed little surprise to see this young flower closing at evening had so many teeth.

All this you thresh out on the floor of your mental granary, the images raining like wheat, trying to figure what it means as suddenly the ship tosses and bucks shaken by seastorm. This too quickly passes in an hour or two, then the green coolness of evening asserts itself again. Calm scudding.

A naked figure floated
        past you on the vast sea
turning turning in sunlight
           weaving the light against it
the waters trying its mouth
        then jettisoned out like a sea spout
by the cold voice rising
        deep from breast cavity
'America my nation
        Egypt is my destination.'

Shoreward the port sails into view and almost floors you, the small craft grinding their way over bumpy seas carrying men brown as evening, not even the evening, her dusky negligee, birds fluttering up out of magicians' mouth on dock, palm trees shooting up along the shoreline quivering gently over the calm scurrying of city.

Egypt is like nothing you have seen. You bury the seed of its vision and its ultimate meaning deep inside you where it can grow unhampered finally to become fruit and tree: until the day of reckoning when the diaphragm of sky heaves out then contracting in again, shows you the thing begun so long ago now visible to you in all its newborn nakedness—Until that day you must go through Alexandria like a face without a body, seeing, yet not seeing and certainly not being seen, not understanding nor knowing the contour but only as shaped from without, knowing its leavings, its excrement, the waste it's become, but never the thing as it must be. It is like the black veil of the fruitseller which she now raises to thank you revealing a gullet completely void of teeth, from which flies file swiftly in retreat, a curtain whose calm outer mystery you can accept, but once lifted contains possibilities you did not expect.

You pass quickly from Alexandria to Cairo, taking the train that very morning. The landscape is just as you conceived it, just as it appeared to you in dreams

the carnival sunlight whirling down
            the magician's blue oxen
turning granaries
      cotton cold as snow
            cloaking scarecrow fields

Perhaps this is what Garvey saw. From this fairytale world he tried to fashion a reality, but a reality that could only be accomplished in a land of dreams where everyone is as they say they are and even transition from homebody to hydra is anticipated in the scheme of things.

We haven't learned our lesson yet. Even Baraka's announcing "We are an African people," suggests that we could skip wantonly over the blossoming, stripping ourselves of niggerness by a decree without once undertaking the agony of this voyage. We are not angels, who gently unzipping our skin can step out of the old life into the new without even the pain of detaching the tarnished wings flapping uncomfortably about our shoulders and depositing them in a garbage can.

Nevertheless your being here obligates you to receive this farout country as they receive you, without caution and without fear as Lazarus must have been received returning dully to the land of the living. To them you have left only a spell ago and they are there to greet you, glad to see you safe on your return; pointing out to you the hotel in which you'll stay and waiting patiently for your release as though you had them under pay, refusing to go even then until you say you will join them later to view *your* city, not as tourist, of course, but as you knew it once, even if you have difficulty bringing the recollection to mind, even if you can't distinguish it from this life or the one you left behind.

You stop in your hotel long enough to leave your luggage at the foot of the bed and admire how swell the view is before you're part of it, given over to it like a painter's landscape when suddenly he sees himself take shape and what was landscape becomes self portrait. Before it was exterior, tableau, now it is world, the soil rising and dying on which you daily go. The tram shuddering squeakily up breakneck hill with limbs lumbering out of window, brings you to the sprawling suburbs behind which lies the desert. This is your first encounter with the desert and its numberless recesses. The Arab music drifts by you, passes through you as you pull slowly near the pyramids. A dancer yearns toward you from kindling fire, gaudier than a gypsy's dream of woe. Yet you continue through this dilapidated backward suburb on out of time. You have met the desert and its sands dance under your feet, then fly before you like a vast eternity.

Here, too, a guide approaches you, negotiating briefly for the view, he peels off beckoning you to follow, poking his stick in the sands before him as though he thought an answer would suddenly rear its head and flick its forked tongue telling him all before it scurried under rock or stone.

"Those are the pyramids, one for each season. We call this the spring, observe its windy vaulting as though momentarily it shall burst into bloom. Come here, into the coolness of its sepulcher, darker than Juliet's tomb. There is the home of the Pharaoh, Rameses II, below him the Jews like black birds lie interred. Still, though your eyes flick quick as a salamander's, the arrow of easy credit slays a thousand niggers.

"The crocodile-shapes along the wall are symbols of the Nile. The boat you see is made of bark which the crocodiles fear to eat. And there where the black blood eats the grass away, lay the sacrifice to Attis."

You can make little of this hieroglyphic muddle. The guide departs leaving you befuddled. You are alone. A bone-chillness bites through you though the evening is still soft and lean. The shadow of history stretches before you like a keyboard. Your fingers are too short to play their ivory chords. You sink back into your old self and its attendant humiliation remembering the sun sinking into the Mississippi as the sky turns yellow and a cluster of slaves around a fire sing out soft and mellow

O deep deep river
  My home is over Jordan

You turn abruptly to go, almost like a woman turns holding a pink bouquet and walks away. You would leave it all behind you did not the Sphinx standing luminously before you obstruct your retreat. This is not the first time it has seen the soul writhing at nightfall, gathering the desert in its arms as the darkness clings to it. It has seen Malcolm and King, starting from different points on the road and gradually unfolding, reach the merging path where retreat becomes impossible and they must either face the moment or pass beyond it into eternity. Not the eternity where cosmic being and 'me' finally merge, but the dull sterile stretch of day where you exist in a funky uxorious gray unable to die completely because you are not alive and unable to live because you cannot accept the thought of dying. They weathered the desert and from it took its meaning.

You too have learned to meet the desert on its own terms, giving nothing, but like the dead sea taking in everything. There will be plenty of time to give later whatever it is you've learned, as soon as the process has taken root in you, when it has become reflex, for actually it's only just begun, is only bud, minerals and soil but not the great flowering tree, nor shall it be until a new you continuously lift its head sending the old selves reeling like dead leaves.

The Sphinx who has sat silently through this entire labor serving only as catalyst to traumatize your two halves and draw them slowly together until they're finally whole, ready to greet the world, remains silent. Yet somewhere out of the vast desert the voice exhorts you

"What time has taken away
                it must give back again."

. . . . .

The white huntress rose from her chair blithely as cork rising from the seaspray and walking wantonly toward the door, paused as the gold of moonlight gathered against her, saying, "It is time, I've stayed too long."

She rises at dawn to feed the swans, at evening she hunts the menacing black boar, with flashlight probing the forest or stalking the string of fishing villages along the Nile.

She is both huntress and quarry, or would be if her snag-toothed star could only illuminate the place where her destiny, already fated to be, since that day love flung wantonly out of a seashell, would plunge through her, not once pausing as she danced whitely beneath the moon.

"To Luxor," the voice urged her, "to Luxor." Her eyes slid open like Venetian blinds. She bathed in the Nile, sublime in the hard sunlight of morning breaking against her waist, then left the forest dragging behind her all that primordial guilt like blind baggage to thump along the night train. It was not her guilt, of course, but that inherited like an old birthright when she was Aphrodite whiling away the afternoon beneath a tree in the forest reading *Moby Dick,* or hunting that old bear with a stick.

Now facing the boar with its black snout filling her with love and fear, she might become it, might through empathy assume the pain of being quarry, spreading herself open to her harsh fate as at her back rough winds sheared the lilies from their stalks.

Like the boar, she too was in exile, a sacred whore to whom all jacks come sometime, climbing through the vegetation to where she lay supine. She sacrificed all. Paris in the spring, Vienna in summer, Switzerland in winter where she slid downhill tumbling into snow, that she might become sacrifice, not even turning once like Lot's wife to consider whether or not she was right. The vernal equinox where night balanced day was only an evening away. She must find him, her rough quarry, must fly to him while she is young with strength left in her fingers and her stumbling voice can still say, her white arms still clothed in moonlight, "I'm sorry, you poor dear. This is my body. Do with it what you will."

. . . . .

To Luxor you've come, a heap of quivering flesh, meshed in the train's rickety-rack along the single track, where turbaned Arabs trading courtesies with you, exchanged a pomegranate for a cold potato.

> An old dodge in a ditch
> Horses so thin their skeletons
> curve round their skin,
> their lips oceans,
> trot through afternoon

Those are impressions as you felt them then, surging, churning, burning in you and begging to be put down as

images from your past rushed on you, and you sucked them clean as a bone. The dead king searching the shore of the Nile for the perfect ebony figure. The hanged man drenched with gasoline and set aflame down in Mississippi. And the grass that year grew green as fire, the cotton heaped high as the Alps and an old man covered with wheat rose out of the river wet with water and ambergris. All this filed past you sorting itself out in your feeling, already frayed from the journey.

Embalmed Luxor spreads out before you bound in filthy bandages. Mummified Luxor where every monument and stone has majesty, still as it was when Jesus was a boy and artisans fashioned their blazed vision, a maze where even lifeless bodies escape derision. And if its bony feet elude the gaze of history, you must remember, this *mummy* that you see is yours.

Your guide and you descend at cliff's end to the waiting ferryboat below. Day gently divides itself halfway between morning and evening. The shroud sails, swollen, drift mysteriously across the Nile, the boat's engine throbbing

BLACK ANIMA

For a long time you've traveled in two separate worlds. There was the land from which you came, calm and vibrant like a double swirl of flutes drowned by the burst of mandolins: and there was the world of Whitey with its three-button-suits and revolutions over the price of tea. Both clashed in you, pulling and pulled with equal passion, stalemated in you. Splay of sea spray. Europe is a shallow grave strewn with mushrooms and Africa a miracle calculating a time to be. But what concerns you immediately is not the coming glory or that we find favor in our obituary—what concerns us is *now*, and that eternally.

It occurred to you that with true being out of the question, given your past, your general direction and incapacity for self-deception, integrity lay in turning without regret and opening the exit, closing the door behind you. Then a new thought pushed its way through the debris cluttering the mental city, to put your memory of the past behind you like yesterday's pin-up girls and start it all again; to stand naked at the threshold of beginning where behind your back cold clouds hang heavily threatening rain, while before you the absence of memory shows you your room as though it, too, has been made anew, as though the chairs, lamps and tables placed on the lawn were rising to greet you.

Only in abiding, in our dogged fidelity to dowdy habits does the decay dig in erecting its monument between pure and unwatched cosmic being and the small unobtrusive self that grasps its meaning, that churns it, carries it on its back like the hump of a camel.

Always begin anew the task that's too much for you. Fling abiding from your arms like a washed-out sea shell. Swallow the long-legged sun swirling down to you. Strip naked on the shore and resolutely in your clay, dance, dance, dance I say. . . .

You heard that voice crossing Lenox Avenue whose cheap neon light fortold no portent of the pilgrim's moon, promising only a different light to steer by, which compass couldn't guess, or sextant contrive; for to reach this sacred city you must lose yourself, abandon yourself to the other more godly possibility in you, leaving the familiar avenue, suddenly startled by the noise of birds and the washed-out haze of starlight soft and dazzling like the light of dreams.

Being Black is not easy. It is more than just the capacity to die whether or not the darkness has stilled your feet, more than a name checks are mailed to, more than a mad shout unheard as moon's music or stars' tingle, more than an ass for the boot. Being Black is full of catching up to our destiny, full of sinew tightening to a scream, full of black veins pulsating with being. Be firmly what you wish to be, wish to be firmly what you are. Cling to the depth within you, that drives you, turns you, like some old bird-god consuming itself to be more fully what it is.

This, too, means beginning, putting the past behind you like a broken thing and striking out on lonely roads un-peopled because unknown, fury roads lit by orange embers of neon sunlight, kinetic clouds kindle as though the sun itself has died, road stricken by the harsh reality of the sky.

Each beginning is an ending, a space we left off long ago like the dust of yesterday crushed under the voyager's feet. We cannot renounce the past without becoming it, unless our star attenuates what in principle we hate. That is why, I suppose, the first phase always involves proving ourselves, assuming the enemy's mask.

The night reveals to you so clearly what Chesnutt and Wheatley were about, the menacing glances cast at the Other as they strained like children to receive more atten-tion than their brothers, not content to express humanity, but becoming what ideally the Other thought life should be. It should therefore not cause us wonder that they slipped beyond the border of who they were to find their despair in an isolated country somewhere between the bickering of Whitey's dream world and the songs of slave camps scintillating the atmosphere so that the evening sifted down and only an ember remained, not even an ember but the ashes of a dream they were no closer to obtaining.

That is why it makes little sense really to start here. We must begin at the beginning the monstrous stretch of sea where Marmaduke and Captain Jope churned their way from the 'dark continent' bringing the first shipment of nonentities. It does little good to condemn the dead for what undoubtedly had to be like the sun coming up each day and almost inciting the old clouds to riot. We cannot argue with destiny and its inevitable accidents that pick its moments for coming like a master criminal picks a burglar-proof lock. Yet, neither should we condemn with sackcloth and weeping the friendly dialectic that shocks Justice out of her sleeping and substitutes new meaning in the place of the old.

To be as these, on totally familiar ground where the flowers know you and gently incline themselves to you, accustomed to the land and its idiosyncrasies and so bored by the stinking waterhole you must defend you could easily scream and walk away abandoning it to the onrushing enemy, who was an otherwise friendly tribe, except for their incessant going on about their manifest destiny, has happened at least once a year from the beginning of man's residence here until the present day. Even Vietnam is a war concerned with water rights and rice. But to them, our forefathers, accustomed to the nonsense that only high breeding and what we absurdly call progress bring, having seen Gonga Mussa pilgrimaging to Mecca and the intellectual fury at Timbuktu, the shock of capture must have seemed a nightmare too protracted to awaken to.

For these the long dream was just beginning, compressed fear contracted into itself like a cluster of wings, imperial prerogatives receded into gradual complacency. God's trumpet failed. The strange men from far away, with skin colored like burial mask or a dread disease when life has left the body, had their way with them, beating them to their knees, snatching their humanity by degrees, until there was only the husk of body to mark the place where a man had breathed.

To many, these white creatures with their germs and their gin must have conformed more closely to what the end should be than we, dying in rented flats and unheated tenements that even the rats abandoned long ago, could possibly hope for. This didn't stop them, I suppose, from expecting sanity to stop lounging about and suddenly shake herself free of these proceedings like an old bitch shedding fleas, or a hostile sky to impatiently flash fiery instructions: Let These People Go.

But the stench of the slave galleys, their terror and their disease convinced them that, though their knees ached with supplicating, only Satan was on their case. From this point of fixed gravity, the Black Muslims are hardly far afield in their characterization of Whitey. Imagine suffering so extreme men leaped joyfully to the waiting sharks that followed the ships as pilgrims pursue their star. Even "seasoning" could have added little to the unreality of this passage. Except for thirst, hunger and the natural drives the flesh is heir to, they had died.

There was only the shame. The shame of capture. The shame of slavery. The shame of not choosing not to be.

Beginning here at our very nadir, where the bellow of confused voices sifts down to you through the inexorable centuries like a deluge of pain, we see plainly that any attempt to rectify the past either by petition or proclamation is doomed to failure like Chamberlain at the line, or a peg-legged man becoming a champion sprinter. We must hollow out a place for ourselves consistent with what we are, yet bearing nothing of our disgrace except such traces by which a downhill climber might reconstruct our upward arc, casting away all dispersions of security and even our names, if need be, like the winds of our breaths in a hurricane.

This is not the first time you have spent another dawnless night hunched over the hot patch of your existence, arranging and rearranging it, trying to scratch some meaning from the rented plot the owner has leased you. These are pygmies standing in a row. These twisted thorns from which the roses wrestle to get free are penitentiaries. And these nightclimbers are stretching themselves to reach the valley of lilies.

It is all there. Working by flashlight you cleave each husk of meaning from its sheaf, or at least what you think is meaning which frequently turns out to be only new questions discarded in the striptease of reality. Yet, taking the river's rhythm as your own, you examine each piece of shrubbery, each tree until dawn collapses on its knees. You pause at daybreak staring the moment calmly through and through, tracing each vein that might lead somewhere, yet leaves you where you were, each hollowing that may contain some hidden meaning, yet never does.

Neither DuBois nor Johnson got beyond the deception this phase is heir to. Just as the son's questions are seldom resolved in the father, but abandoned along the roadside to find new questioners, our forefathers of the twenties inquire, "What does it all mean, this being Black?" and hearing no answer set on their way. All this might have revealed something new, did not the unanswered question continuously impose itself to blot out the view?

Yet because of such forefathers and forefathers like these, the forest has gradually detached itself from the cluster of trees around it. It is now evident that the Other, i.e. Whitey, no longer needs to flay our skin until it drapes about our knees, what he would do to us, we do unconsciously to ourselves and our brothers. Not that we abide out and out suicide, far from it. We must mask our despair drinking warm whiskey from the silver volcano some rich Westchester Jew imported and bottled especially for you, or plunging needles into our skin we gracefully perform the death-dance of heroin at the local music academy Whitey has rented for the night.

Of this, too, our forefathers were guilty. To have leaped to God, Africa, or the Communist party thereby gently detaching themselves from the reality of their brothers was worse than diving off top balconies. Richard was right, there is no help for pain, nothing to take for our suffering, but doggedly remembering who we are and thus detaching ourselves from the various dependencies that engulf us. That is why what we mistakenly call power in his work is only a need to murder the calender of wings obstructing our mobility. We must empty ourselves of hope, free our spirits from the long vomit of centuries. Only through murdering hope can hope be.

All this became clear to you
At the Apollo Theater one night
with hip soul sisters' hysterical swooning
as cobalt frames burn on a reel.

Narcissus enters wantonly on the screen
wearing neon hotpants,
sipping martinis and flirts with queen
over porcelain rim of glass.

Zeus is hot for him
this divine begetter climbs imperviously.
Youth admires his godly physique
richly clothed in the moddest fashions:
the god is graceful, daring
yet never flashy, never
submitting to a servile passion.

Mystically he extends his immortal hand
the youth accepts masking his joy as best he can
exit the lovers through the vulgar crowd
to take their pleasure in an old sedan

Wright knew it all, knew all this scene, how Black youth
amazed by such flamboyancy might mistake the boredom
of these two for an existential glory. With both Hitler and
Skinner still becoming, he knew nevertheless, that foul
crew had set us dribbling like a dog. Whitey, just as Zeus,
had his penis in our asses, though each Sunday the Lord
would bring, there were emissaries paid to condemn our
lack of virginity.

That's why Baldwin after him, accustomed to things slid-
ing in and out, became our spokesman. In that startingly
beautiful alabaster scene where the calm was only shattered by a pair of marvelous wings whipping their way

across the sky, and the sonorous voice of Bessie Smith like the swirl of a bass bassoon, he reconciled himself to being Black, homosexual, and ugly. Nor shall we, after him, elude the thousand idiosyncrasies a colonized people in their mother country have acquired naturally.

All this, you insist is ancient history. What has this to do with the price of sniffing-glue in Rainwater, Mississippi? Just this:

We are only a bridge connecting the rose of the future with the disappointment of yesterday. The moonlight made of corduroy will shine across your ebony body as is its destiny, but for the living, we to whom things happen and who, thank God, can make things happen in return, to burn the past either by petition or ignoring its meaning will destroy the main support, hurling us headlong into unexplored spaces we never dreamed. Even if these spaces are essentially friendly, we can take nothing from them, having nothing by which to measure whatever treasure heart holds dear, or mind finds, but like babies are reduced to touch and taste.

We can hardly afford in-fighting, not with the dead, for, since they can no longer defend themselves, we must be the defense for them, and certainly not with the living who momentarily passed from grace, since it is almost certain someday we shall take their place. Being Black requires the support of all, both the living and the dead, and what's more, the love of whoever, Blue, Black, White or Green, has, either from ambition or shame, counted himself on humanity's team. Those who from sheer hatred scream militancy, unable to conceive a definitive orgasm, have left to them only the shriveled head of a wet dream.

Thus as the miles slide under your feet you come at evening to a clearing in Riverside park where meaning threatens to divulge itself were it not for the wrinkled white whore staring you face to face.

Cast the bitch behind you that blocks the view, be the song you sing, the melody and the source. For when wouldn't a vision stay, restrain its parting, as you, free at last, come into the open? A choir of gospel singers attend your coming. The light pierces your dusty skin, the blackness shining through and through: you are the radiant darkness which at nightfall the traveler comes home to. You are the breath of spring for which the swallows are waiting.

Yet even in this opening where suddenly you realize who you are, the light engulfing you, buoying you up fresh and free full of pure being, an older, colder voice has left harsh questions in isolate spaces you now occupy without fear.

In throwing off deception you deceive yourself again. All life is illusion, pain. There is no joy, no happiness, no help for suffering. Get all the money you can, life abhors a vacuous, serving man.

Hearing this voice spring's harbinger begins receding along the single track. The calm is shattered, while at your back swallows weave indecipherable calligraphy. The opening so clearly before you shuts like a lid leaving only streaks of light that might be eyes. You must rescue the vision or die, not real death perhaps, but relapse into that old complacency.

Are you ready to begin again having seen the other for the first time stripped naked as he is, his slimy reptilian skin starting at the feet and stopping where the sex begins? This immodest creature so caught up with his own being that, though the water frightened by his ugly face fled along the orange rim of the sky, still stands there admiring himself in a mirror he's constructed in the mud. This is what you once envied, strove to become, pushing your past gently behind you like the stones under the climber's feet.

Listen my heart, hear the music drifting to you as suddenly the opening turns on you like a smile, radiant and carefree as if it had been there all the while. The Other is behind you now, stretched in the shadow of his blood like some awful dragon. Perhaps this was part of the process, that you could come more completely to stand beside yourself, to be. Shall you follow the music of the blue outward sky lightening across the horizon like the ghetto shaking a handful of sunflowers?

Up, up along the Hudson, across the highway, the screaming of whistles, the noise of tambourines stinging the atmosphere. Everything is everything. The mind-melting music urging the diving swallows down, the upshooting grass, man building sky and wing merged in one violent glowing. All is touched by flame, though no flame singes a single thing. A sort of glory has descended like a hurricane of fine flame.

_____

Broadway is wearing a vest of lights. The dance is in progress as the dancers urge you onward, clapping, spinning, clapping. Colors flash, bright orange and blue. A bit of green swirls by. Harlem is beautiful as it can only be in dreams. An old man covered with mushrooms bops toward you weaving, turning, weaving. He beckons you, you follow, the noise of tambourines and whistling nearer, nearer, nearer, my God, to you. Up the smooth tenement stair, the stoop lights give you the eye as you dance past them. You enter the first door on the right. Clash of cymbals. Swirling strobe lights.

The crazy flopping dance climbed to such fury, your soul sailed out of your skin like lunar landing gear leaving the craft behind. You forbear these cries of ecstasy calmly as though hurled in a hurricane's eye, for now you see, despite the tambourines, the whistling, the mad screams mounting to a crescendo of euphoric vision, it is only a scene like thousands you have witnessed before. The mother reclining on a cushioned sofa, queen of Harlem for a day, abandons her sorrow at evening while her children and her children's children dance wildly about her. But the moment's meaning burst beyond its average place to where the common and the cosmic have meeting, the fabled mid-winter spring where as simple an act as opening up the hand reveals a master plan, the unseen proddings that we die and live by.

The vision of the strange euphoric family where harmony has grown so great each dies the other's death and lives the other's fate, has set you muttering like an ass.

Our prophets tell us
that only by fasting and prayer
can men beget a vision
of the holy stair,
but here excess of being is wrought
to such elation
both hell and heaven come into relation.

I see so clearly what we
by picketing and protest demand
is but a fragment
of what spiritual man
fumbling, stumbling, frolicking
to and fro, cut off from Nature
and her master branch,
needs to make him grow.

That old dichotomy of soul and body's
not so sacred as they used to say
our political salvation
and our spiritual command
both require we love our fellowman,
what more is there to say?

Even a militant should not have murder as his ultimate
end, no matter how his body tenses to knock the thrust
away, shatter the rib-cage and snatch that strange heart
beating where it lay. The world is shrinking, the planets
pulling closer day by day. Abiding now is certain death.
Man must cling cautiously to what he knows best, the rest
we take from Nature. We're not of one a kind, not of one
spirit as the salmon that know their way upstream, accept-
ing all the consequence of birth and death, never ques-
tioning, as though death itself were but the necessary cul-
mination of a dream.

But we are surfeited. Everything is drifting, drifting. Not for a single second do we have pure spring in which the roses know themselves and grow without the strangling smog whirling down to choke them. We are biologically insane and only this dance can make us well again, syncopating our rhythms with nature's own, wrenching free of the death within us, grown so comfortable it would be shocked by an increase of being. Strip naked in that room as the music summons you to do, caress the dancing girl her hair heavy with cornrows and swing, swing until the morning comes sifting down.

I don't know much about families, but I do know that without the unity we have seen we can only witness spring's lament, but never the spring itself, the rain plunging to the black earth, but never the time flowers assert themselves, glad to be part of Mother Earth. Without this great anima rooted in herself like a glorious tree while her children dance pneumatically about her like a maniac storm of leaves, the fruit would have rested in the womb and Harlem absent of its queen might have been swept away by the storm.

We cannot stop here. When illegitimacy or thumbing one's nose at the community are out of the question, we must make more fully ours the vision until its veins run in our collective veins and its black blood has commerce with ours. The tree has turned to Daphne, the gentle queen of noble bearing, as they said it would, she who, having been tree accepts more fully her people's destiny and is content to be the source from which all goodness springs.

It is not easy taking on new ways having accepted so securely the old way of doing things, to become music vibrating in harmony like the strings of a mandolin, when accustomed to being noise. The clock knocks along its course so eagerly that we hardly have the time to get used to what must be, or grieve properly for what we leave behind, before the old proddings are marshaling us again. We must answer its incessant ticking with a working of our own, not weighing what we personally will profit, but if those we love enough to underwrite as beneficiaries will think our struggling as important as we. Whether leaf, branch or bole, we belong to the same tree. May it spread over Harlem like a great blooming laurel.

How can she blame you then, she, the guardian of the future unity you have imagined and half imagined, if through reciprocity her daughter and you, ignorant of all except the pain clawing in you like a leopard, decide to seal this memory and live together. Black Eurydice no more, the visions of Malcolm and King would have a happy ending if you could touch her down where all sources spring. Family, unity and this new beginning we have adumbrated for ourselves are not dichotomies, but symbolically come together where flesh lingers, sometimes staying for the night.

We are ripped apart from the natural world and can only reassert ourselves by behaving naturally. We say soul, God and poetry for the manifest Being that shakes us utterly, yet should these presences greet each other it's only to say farewell. The dance has grown madder, the music more intense, but you no longer notice since they've become experience in you, imprinted in the circulation of the lymph. The dance you both do, the bugaloo, the penguin or any other funky, mean, lowdown, swinging thing, flings aside these old categories of being like the air that was yesterday's, leaving only their breaths, the spring that they were but could never achieve, being so bogged down, so enamored of their name and the shades of hidden meaning. There is only the flame of their passion, not even a flame, a single burning that encompasses all. The *All is all and all is All*, demanding of the tree as well as of whatever is flying or hates the stationary that they exist in her. So in this dance, battered blood circulates beyond our fear of whatever's cheap or transitory and sands dance at the wedding of the years.

It would seem, seeing how sweet's the braided girl that drives your blood, some sort of ceremony's demanded to commemorate the dream made flesh, the new beginning that reestablished itself in the dancer bopping before you like a lantern throwing patterns on the ceiling. Let the birthday party and its bright festive mood become the marriage feast, the public testimony of the immediate transformation she wrought in you. For you have seen it all, all presenting itself to you not flamboyantly scribbling itself across the evening in archaic calligraphy like a gold tooth in the mouth of a Nashville Negro, but subtly shaping itself in you, waiting this exact moment and this year to manifest itself for you to see, as long ago in the confusion of scribbling you first recognized your name.

What the moment has given cannot be spoken of in your biography or eulogized by beefy banquet speakers, for it is only a way of forgetting, of postponing the past that presses you too closely to grasp its meaning, allowing you to develop freely, cultivating corrective vision that will thrust you into the dizzy heights from which you can survey all your valley. But forgetting is only the beginning, a small turn in the brain's combustion system. You must know how to wait until memory seeks and exhausts herself in you. Thus putting aside your Blackness momentarily, you grow, discovering a black identity the fashionable publicity sheets neither imagine nor know.

But to move beyond this process to what really concerns us dearly, forgetting further connects us with the Ground of Being, permitting us participation in an Eternal Now in which the roses are always unfolding, while what we were formerly, but should not have been, is eternally forgotten. We see now more clearly what King implied, the real meaning of this dance and all it symbolizes, our spiritual and racial salvation are wedded more closely than rain's wetness. For, just as we cannot unpeel white from snow, we cannot divorce bigotry, man's turning away from humanity, from sin, man's turning from the face of God. This too was prefigured in the dance, binding the transitory body to a soul in which all the old archetypes flutter about in their accustomed way.

All this was woven upon the symbolic ring you placed around her finger. See, there is Eve and Adam leaving the cluster of palm trees turning violently from the light which hotly pursues them. And here, Cinquez, hands chained to side, averting with downcast eyes the swirling sunlight. And here Malcolm and King each shaking hands while pointing toward the single pathway where the sun sinks behind the row of trees. And here are we, this space glowing festively is the room, these are the dancers pressing us so closely and here, the mother raising her hand to bless.

Still, secure in this knowledge the stars shine more intensely over Harlem as though to give back what time has taken away. You and the marriage party dance naked down Broadway, unconcerned about the weather or what the day will bring.

NOTES

Changes

One

PAGE 5   KING.   Dr. Martin Luther King.

PAGE 6   GONGA MUSSA.   Gonga Mussa ruled the famed Melle Kingdom at its height. His historic pilgrimage to Mecca was both a lavish, almost barbaric display of wealth and a symbol of the heights of African culture.

PAGE 5   MALCOLM.   Malcolm X.

PAGE 6   CINQUEZ.   The leader of the famous Amistad revolt. The Amistad was a slaver bound for Cuba. Cinquez assumed control of the vessel with the Spanish at his mercy. The ship arrived in America where a great debate ensued as to whether or not Cinquez or his men should be allowed to return to Africa or forced to proceed to Cuba. They were eventually released to return to Africa.

PAGE 28   SEVENTH SON.   In *The Souls of Black Folk* DuBois writes:

> After the Egyptian and Indian, the Greek and Roman, the Teuton and Mongolian, the Negro is a sort of seventh son, born with a veil, and gifted with second-sight in this American world. . . .

PAGE 28   IN "A Litany of Atlanta," DUBOIS WRITES:

> Thou art not dead, but flown afar
>   up hills of endless
> light through blazing corridors
>   of suns . . .

PAGE 28   BONE.   Robert Bone who in *The Negro Novel In America* asks of DuBois, "what sort of empathy could this young intellectual feel for the black masses who, like Zora, are cursed with the heritage of slavery?"

Eight

PAGE 30   HUGHES.   Langston Hughes, "The Negro Speaks Of Rivers."

PAGE 30   CRISES.   Major magazine of the "Harlem Renaissance." The magazine was edited by DuBois and introduced a number of young poets including Hughes.

PAGE 30   ROSY.   Rosy Pool. Translated *The Diary of Ann Frank*. She was one of the first whites in London to edit an anthology of Black writing called *Beyond The Blues*.

PAGE 31   TOLSON.   Melvin Tolson whose "Harlem Gallery" is a major work.

PAGE 31   LENNY HORN.   Lawrence C. Horn who wrote a

very promising book of poems that has remained unpublished.

PAGE 31   IKHNATON.   Ikhnaton was an Egyptian pharaoh who established the first monotheistic religion. Freud thought that Moses was a disciple of Ikhnaton. If this is true, there is only one religious line beginning with Aton, the sungod whom Ikhnaton worshiped, and ending with either Christ or Mohammed, depending on one's point of view.

PAGE 31   CHARLES WADDELL CHESNUTT.   First major Black prose writer.

PAGE 32   MPHAHLELE.   Ezekiel Mphahlele is a South African Black and critic of literature. He is author of *The African Image*.

PAGE 32   JOSEPH.   Joseph Conrad.

PAGE 32   QUEEN VICKY.   Queen Victoria.

PAGE 33   MARLOWE.   The narrator and surrogate for the author in Conrad's stories. In *The Heart of Darkness* Marlowe says:

> The conquest of the earth, which mostly means the taking it away from those who have a different complexion or slightly flatter noses than ourselves, is not a pretty thing when you look into it too much. What redeems it is the idea only. An idea at the back of it, not a sentimental belief in the idea—something you can set up, and bow down before, and offer a sacrifice to. . . .

PAGE 33   PROSPERO.   Shakespeare's *Tempest*. O. Mannoni has recognized the essential colonialism within the play. In his interpretation, Prospero is, of course, the colonialist and Caliban the rebellious native.

thou who hast no foes
I am thy sister, whom thou lovest;
thou shalt not part from me.

Sixteen

Seventeen

116

Birth and Rebirth *and* **Black Anima**

I have borrowed heavily from Frazer's *Golden Bough*, combining myths as it seemed to my advantage. The two most important ones here are those of Aphrodite and Osiris, which I have purposely melded with the modern sexual myths of Black-White relationships. Aphrodite is love turned huntress searching for the image of her beloved (Adonis) in the wild boar, which she fears. The figures of lover and huntress for her are, in fact, inseparable. She is at once Aphrodite, the sacred prostitute and Isis, the beautiful Egyptian goddess searching for her lover-brother. She is the promise of renewal, yet she remains only promise. What time has taken away it must give back again. It is, therefore, only in the Black Anima that the poem's central figure can be fused to a single unified vision.

NORMAN J. LOFTIS was born in Chicago in 1943. He has lived in New York for seven years and took his Ph.D. at Columbia University. He has traveled widely in Europe and the Middle East. His first book of poems, *Exiles and Voyages,* was published by Black Market Press in 1970. Mr. Loftis teaches English at Hunter College in the City University of New York. He lives on Central Park West with his wife and four children.

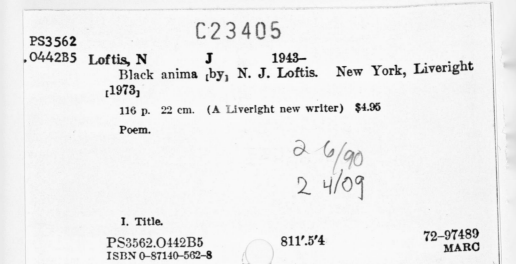